D0910965

santa rosa

Wendy McGrath

a novel

SANTA ROSA

NeWest Press

Library and Archives Canada Cataloguing in Publication

McGrath, Wendy
Santa Rosa / Wendy McGrath.
ISBN 978-1-897126-81-3
I. Title.
PS8575.G74S26 2011 C811'.6 C2010-906767-3

Editor: Douglas Barbour
Book design: Natalie Olsen, Kisscut Design
Author photo: John McGrath

NeWest Press acknowledges the support of the Canada Council for the Arts, the Alberta Foundation for the Arts, and the Edmonton Arts Council for our publishing program. We acknowledge the financial support of the Government of Canada through the Canada Book Fund for our publishing activities.

NeWest Press
#201, 8540 – 109 Street
Edmonton, AB T6G 1E6
780.432.9427
www.newestpress.com

No bison were harmed in the making of this book.

printed and bound in Canada 1 2 3 4 5 13 12 11 1

for John

as white light runs past
like a dog,
where did it go?
where did it all go?

CHARLES BUKOWSKI, "bent"

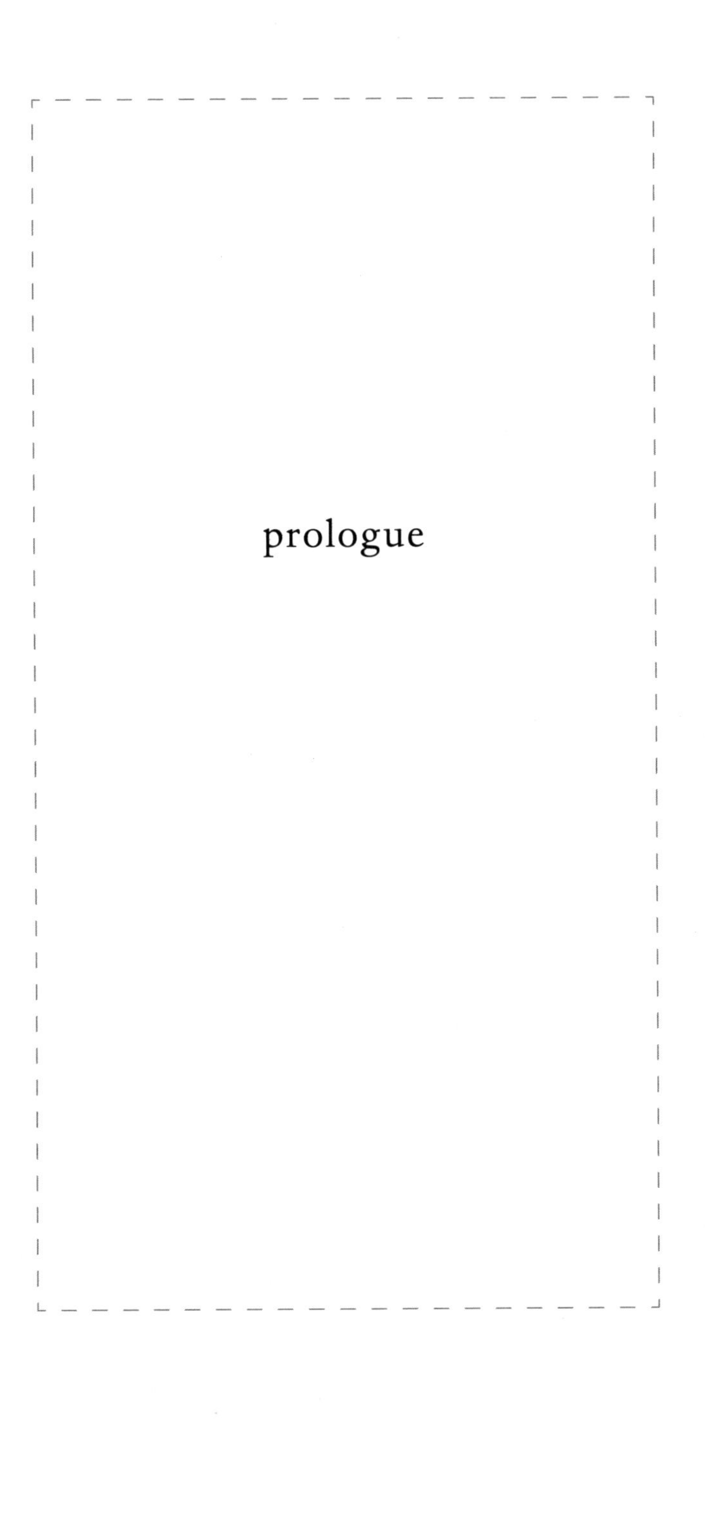

prologue

when christine discovered she was pregnant she began
to crave the taste of dirt   her sense of smell of taste
of touch was keener than it had ever been   in malls
she smelled cigarette smoke when she couldn't even
see a cigarette   positive she tasted vinegar in chicken
soup   she was able to detect the slightest variation
in the taste of water   she smelled dust   tea stains
in the sink

in a book of days she kept track of what she ate how
many glasses of milk she drank whether or not she had
taken a vitamin pill   all these details became infinitely
important   each day a remembrance

february   her garden plot in the middle of the
backyard was hidden under snow   after five years it
was well worked no shade perfectly flat   the ground
melted quickly in spring and froze just as quickly in fall
this time of winter   the same month they found out
the baby was coming   the plot looked like nothing
at all   invisible   sleeping   yet she knew the soil
underneath that thick layer of snow was sumptuous
she wouldn't be too big to work soil   plant seeds
by the time the ground thawed   this year she was
impatient to get into her garden

nine months seemed a very long time   long enough
to get prepared she thought   although how prepared
can you really be   christmas lights still dangled
from their sad looking elm tree in the front yard
she and fergal would have to start thinking about
things like that   when you have a baby you have
to have some sort of structure   some sort of routine
you can't leave your christmas lights up until easter

elm trees lined both sides of the street and bare and
without leaves they looked like something found
on the brontë moors   bony looking trees   she was
finding it hard to imagine that the soil in her garden
would ever reveal itself but it would appear just as
the baby would appear   patience

what are you doing around the second week in
november she'd asked fergal   they had laughed at the
prospect of what was to come   then they sat across
the kitchen table from each other

ok what do we do now

christine liked to keep houseplants   ivy   coleus
jade plant   when she watered them
she poked at the soil with a fork   allowing the water
to reach the very bottom of the pots   allowing the
smell of the soil to escape to her   damp dark and
unattainable   she tasted the smell of it   smelled the
taste of the dirt

when people found out she was going to have a baby
of course they would ask
any peculiar cravings   a friend's sister had craved
chalk when she was pregnant   another woman craved
the smell of gas and kept the tank of her car full the
whole nine months before

she couldn't understand that at all   even a whiff of gas
fumes made her feel sick

never before had she heard of anyone who had craved
dirt when pregnant   but don't all children eat dirt at
some time or another

her navel was disappearing   her body was becoming
a stranger to her   inverted pear   ice cream cone
number five turned upside down   but she liked
the way she looked   changing into something else
someone else   it became impossible to zip zippers

button buttons she started wearing fergal's clothes
imagined the earth in the garden soften christine
grew rounder as the earth thawed and warmed farther
down

a narrow brown line appeared on her belly *linea nigra*
fergal traced it with his finger kissed it she felt
quickening and as the baby swam inside her thought
of dirt couldn't help it this spring she would turn
the earth in her garden plot and imagine that she was
taking a bite of the ground every time her shovel bit
the soil

raisins currants candied lemon peel red and green
candied cherries had been soaking in napoleon brandy
for exactly seven days jan stirred the fruit
into a batter

cinnamon cloves allspice black currant jam

the cake batter was tinged purple dotted with colour
pointillism
black next to deep brown yellow red green
jan imagined it smelled like the air
of places he had dreamed of caribbean france
maybe ireland didn't currants grow wild there
he poured this mixture into an old battered bundt pan

buttered and floured
let it cook itself over the course of several hours
another pan of water in the oven invisibly invading
adding to the cake itself

the cake cooled on a wood cutting board beside the stove
it was july   the leaves on the trees outside were utterly
still   utterly silent   heat and scent rose from the cake
six months were needed to ripen it
everything is better as it ages   takes on the taste
of what is beside it what contains it what it touches
the fruit in the cake would become the taste of brandy
bark of cinnamon   black currants

next morning he inverted the pan   there were subtle
mounds and valleys which rose and fell gently around
the opening in the cake's middle   he gently stroked
the indentations
the cake curved into itself   it was perfect

he sprinkled brandy like holy water over the cake's
surface and watched it disappear absorbed by the form
of the cake itself   he wrapped it in three layers of
cheesecloth again he sprinkled the cake with brandy
it was then he took the cedar box down from the top
shelf in the pantry just off the kitchen

when it rested on that shelf from january to june
he never looked at it but he thought of it often
he placed the cedar box on the counter beside the
wrapped cake and opened the lid   the scent of last
year's cake still faint inside   smell of brandy
fruit and spice   cedar and earth   that spot in his
back yard where his and his neighbours' fence met
and the earth was protected by the boughs of the
couple's spruce tree   where the soil never froze
completely but stayed
consistently cool through the entire year

the cedar box was thick and he imagined indestructible
he lifted the cake into the box deep   the cake fit exactly
round cake in a square box   yet when he placed the
cake inside he knew its scent would invisibly fill the
spaces left inside the box   he had been correct to
construct a container with right angles straight sides a
tight seal to hold this tradition   his father too had been
a baker but this cake   this recipe he had vowed never
to write down

watch jan he had said   learn by the smell of it
by the weight of it

jan watched his father's hands   the way his fingers moved
the way they coated each piece of fruit with flour and
turned the batter into the pan   for a joke his father
would touch the tip of jan's nose with his index finger

leave a skiff of flour and jan would leave the white dust
there   a kind of magic thing

his father's hands were always smooth   touch   faintly
sweet of apples
bread dough   butter   spices

jan closed the lid of the cedar box   sealing the cake inside
cradling the box he carried it
to the spot in his backyard where the fences meet
where the earth never completely freezes and knelt
there setting the box beside him

see the back of his head   he keeps his hair closely
cropped and trimmed high up the back of his neck
cut straight across because his hair   when allowed   grows
oddly upward on the nape and sticks out as it grows

using a spade he digs a hole deep enough to contain the
box   scrapes the bottom of the hole out with his hands
dirt under the nails of his thick and bent fingers

if he could he would put the earth itself into the cake

smell of the cedar chest of the damp earth
of fruit   brandy   black currants

may   christine and fergal had turned the earth on
the entire garden plot   the middle three months
kneeling awkwardly she reaches for a handful of dirt
curve of her arms created by her reaching   her
beckoning   squeezes the dirt and brings it close to
her nose   but she could not bring herself to eat it
the smell of the dirt made her want it   feel of it in
her mouth   damp humus smell made her want it
she has told fergal about this craving and he thinks
it funny   tells her about a woman back home who
craved salt

christine wants to plant three rows of carrots
coreless amsterdam   royal chantenay   nante
when the carrots grow to the size of fingers she will
start to pick them   eat one straight from the garden
rub the dirt away with her hands   dirt actually part
of the taste of the thing itself   the dirt tastes like the
carrot   carrot like the dirt   everything that grows
underground carries that taste with it   she would
leave the taste of earth on whatever she ate

that night she dreams:

I sit on a wooden bench beside a wooden table and
I recognize the smell of the wood but I can't put a place
to it   my baby is sleeping in my arms but I can't keep
his head up
it keeps falling into the dirt and I keep trying to keep
his head up and I try to wipe his face off with a cloth
I get from beside me on the bench but someone has
used it to wipe the dirt off their boots and I am trying
to find a clean spot on the cloth and try to wipe my
baby's perfect head and I wipe so gently he doesn't wake

there is the smell of the wood and the smell of my baby
I recognize water and air and fire and every element on
earth now and before now

it is july and the garden begins to grow in on itself
green   her craving for dirt is abating

they eat small peppery red radishes   butter lettuce
eat rare beans and save the seeds   ireland creek annie
heirloom seeds the colour of onion skins   calypso
whose seeds look like yin and yang   trout   rorschach
speckled   black   wait for the corn to ripen
its tassles strain to pull earth to sky

and as suddenly as she had the craving for dirt
she loses it

pink marks small scribbles appear on the skin of
her belly the baby kicks and moves she strokes her
stomach automatically

jan makes himself a cup of instant coffee every morning
since astrid died there is no point making a whole pot
on the stove   he pours boiling water over the scratchy
brown granules and waits for the foam and the small
noise it makes in its forming

he thinks of the cake he made those months ago
looks at the space in the pantry left by the box and takes
his hat and coat from the rusty hook by the back door

this year he will carefully wrap and send a piece of
his cake to his youngest daughter in montreal oldest
daughter in yellowknife his son in vancouver
and a piece to the young people next door   they will
appreciate it   by christmas there will be three in that
house   jan is glad to think of the extra noise in their
home   the random noise he would hear from the other
side of his fence

he walks at the same time everyday   summer and winter
early morning when the day still makes promises
lately he has seen his neighbour christine out at the same
time   walking around their yard dead-heading flowers
stooping awkwardly to pull a weed   how are you feeling
when is the baby due again   november
well congratulations
congratulations

one morning on his way back he sees her sitting
in their small glassed-in veranda
she is as close to the small desk in the corner as her belly
will allow and she is writing in a book
her black hair pulled back

her craving for dirt has been replaced by a craving to
pick up her journals again   one for dreams   one for ideas
one for descriptions   christine makes notes
she is writing at the strangest times   sleeps in short
bursts of consciousness   writing down her dreams
when she wakes up

sitting beside her and the beat up roll-top desk that
doesn't roll down fergal asks her
about living in ireland for a while   sell everything
open up a b&b   it would be good for the two of them
the three of them

she becomes absorbed in the images on the outside of
the cup she drinks from   first saw them carved into rock
helix   shape of a stove element burnt on plastic
she traces the shape with her finger   printing the shape
onto her body   shape of infinity on her skin

household articles and natural disasters:

– pots and pans
da Vinci's drawing of utensils raining from the sky
it's also rained frogs before
cats and dogs

– plates
tectonic   seven major   armour they keep trying
to put themselves back together   fault
trying and it's the trying that causes the natural disasters
volcanoes   earthquakes

– forks
lightning   you can still live after you've been hit
but not if you're wet   stay out of open fields
don't seek shelter under a tree

three months to go   three times three is nine
if three is a magic number   then there should be three
times that sense of magic

christine wakes 2:07 august 5 senses something
on the inside of her leg then a sudden release of fluid
there is no pain until she stands up time has stopped
at this point help me fergal they dress quickly in
the dark and forget to lock the door behind them

jan goes for his walk and sees christine's chair at the
desk empty the next three mornings he looks for her
but she isn't there

on the fourth morning he sees their car drive up and
park in front of the house the two of them just sit
there then get out and walk slowly tentatively into
the house as if they have no business being there but
have nowhere else to go

when jan leaves his house the next morning he
wonders what he can possibly offer them   there is
suddenly nothing where everything was   it happens
so quickly
you aren't aware that it's you in the dream

he hesitates at the path leading to christine and fergal's
front door   turns around and goes back into his
house to get his spade   walks to the place where
the box is buried   where the fence and the boughs
of the spruce have made a shelter   digs down and lifts
the box from the earth   there is the smell of cedar
smell of the soil

jan brushes dirt from the top and slowly opens the lid

I

The bathroom of the house was like the inside of a camera.
The tiny room had no window. Dark when the one bulb
above the mirror was off and the door was closed.
This weekday morning she watched her father shaving
but his image lacked a punch black and white contrast.
Flat grey light seeped into the room from the window
in the kitchen on a winter morning simply too cold for
her father to work.

With his left hand he pulled the short string of tiny silver
beads beside the bulb. The sudden brightness turned his
image into negative. A suggestion. He plugged the sink
with a white rubber stopper and turned the silver
on the hot water faucet. A rusty squeak and steam
began to rise.

To the right of the mirror a small medicine cabinet its
handle a wooden thread spool held on with a finishing
nail. He opened the door took out a can of shaving cream
his razor and a small parchment-wrapped package of razor
blades. Dangerous. She had been warned. Cut fingers.
Blood. Lots of blood. Set each to the left of the faucet.

Her father turned the ring on the silver handle and opened
the razor's trap doors. Took a blade from the neat pile
of silver rectangles with successive stacked mouths in
the middle. The little cleft on top the same cleft on the
bottom. They looked smooth and happy.

Once thinking about the razor blades in their case she had gone into the bathroom just to look at them. Closed the door and decided she wanted a closer look and had taken one of the blades from the package. She held it delicately between thumb and forefinger of her right hand. Just to see what would happen she traced a line on the knuckle of her thumb. It didn't bleed right away. It stung first and then red crept to the surface of her skin. She had watched the blood as it gathered itself in tiny dots along the cut line. The girl quietly put the razor blade back where she had found it slowly closing the mirrored door so it wouldn't squeak. She told her mother it was an accident that she had cut herself with one of the knives in the kitchen drawer.

The knife sharpener had come to their neighbourhood just the other day and when he knocked on the front door wearing a beautiful grey coat and tipped his fancy grey hat at the girl's mother she invited him in. He carried a big black case and the girl's mother said What a fine coat and she draped it over her arm smoothed it and hung it on the old hook in the back porch. The knife sharpener joked with the girl's mother Oh I make a decent living. He had spread a purple velvet cloth on the kitchen table. Her mother had given him three of her knives and he had laid them down gently in a row with the sharp side of the blades all pointing the same direction. It reminded the girl of the altar at church. Then he sharpened each knife in turn. The girl could still hear the scrape of the knife sharpener's stone and was glad she hadn't cut her thumb straight through to bone.

The girl's mother wrapped a band-aid around the cut and said Don't worry it will be alright. The girl believed her wanting to tell her about the razor blade and how she had done it on purpose but thought accident sounded better in the end.

Her father took a blade from the package and offered it up to the space under the trap doors. Swivelled the ring on the handle and closed the doors tightly.

As the hot water ran her father shook the can of shaving cream. He shook the can so hard and fast that his lips clenched. The can was a blur of red grey and black. Paint thrown back and forth over and over in the air. The moment cream turns to butter. Thick. He extended two fingers and squeezed out the foam. A clean white t-shirt white foam on his fingers white light above the sink grey light from the kitchen. The round white-bordered mirror with a waning band of steam at the bottom. Negative image.

Her father never simply smeared the shaving cream on his face. He washed his face in water as hot as he could stand and then patted on the foam starting from the cheekbone on the right side of his face down to his square jaw over his chin and moving up to his left cheekbone. He stretched his neck and patted the cream on in short strokes. He kept his mouth tightly closed against the taste. It smelled like lemon and spices a moment pungent and sweet at the same time.

The water in the toilet bowl was clear. She swatted down the toilet lid and stood on it.
She watched her father as the foam peeled away from his face in strips.

Will I ever need to shave Dad? Prb'ly not he said moving his lips as little as possible to keep out the foam. 'nless you turn into the bearded lady and join the circus then you wouldn't be shaving anyway. Wouldn't be able to make a decent living without a beard huh?

Her father's mouth smiled through the white foam his mouth now the same shape as the open space on the razor blades. She laughed too although she was thinking what the knife sharpener and her father said seemed to make sense. The make a decent living part. If she were a bearded lady she would need to make a decent living. She thought everyone must need to make a decent living.

Anyway she didn't want to be a bearded lady when she grew up.

Her parents had taken her and her sister to the fair that past summer. It was a Saturday and her father had gotten up even earlier than usual. He went to work all the way to the west side that morning so they could all go to the fair that very afternoon. When she asked her mother if they could stay until it was dark and the fireworks came on she said maybe. The girl was excited. She wasn't quite sure what went on at a fair but thought it would have something to do with toys and fireworks.

She thought the fair would have something to do with toys because of the dark brown teddy bear that tottered on a three-legged wooden stool in the house. The bear was as big as the girl. Her father had won it for her mother at a fair they went to just after they were married. Her father had to throw baseballs at empty milk bottles and her mother said it cost him more to win it for her than if he had just gone out and bought her a big stuffed bear. That was the way it was then I guess he said.

The fairgrounds weren't far from their house but they drove there because her sister was too small to walk that far. The air was scorching and dry and when the girl slammed the back door of the car the handle was hot. Watch your fingers her mother said.

The picture of the family as they walked the parking lot pavement was overexposed. Taken into the sun. Too bright. Too hot in some spots. The girl could feel the bottoms of her feet begin to warm. She had to squint against the sunlight shining on the chain link fence on either side of the entrance against carnival rides that roiled against the sky against the Ferris wheel an aperture perpetually open on her adventure.

They stood at the wicket as her father and mother talked about the admission charges. Might as well get the family pass her mother said. As her father took a worn black leather wallet out of the back right pocket her mother told him to be careful there are always pickpockets at these places. He put even change from a 20 back into his wallet like he was shuffling cards. To the girl her parents looked like movie stars. Her mother had slept in picks and rollers and her hair was curled and fluffy. She wore bright red lipstick. She had on a white sleeveless blouse and her summer skirt with yellow daisies. Her father had shaved and wore his best short-sleeved shirt. He never wore it to work. Her mother had ironed a crease in his good grey pants and his black shoes shone. They had their arms around each other and staggered for a few steps as they tried to find their balance together. Her father almost tripped but he was laughing as he said Jesus...

Ice Cream Soft Serve the sign said in swirly letters. Who could go for a cone? her father asked. We just got here her mother said but they stood in line and the young man in a red and white uniform watched the ice cream intently as it flowed into three perfect segments and tapered to a curl. Her mother wasn't much for sweet things so she shared her ice cream with her youngest daughter.

The girl rode on a small bike that went around in a circle. She asked for a candy apple which she got. Beautiful red stained glass but it made her think of the evil queen in Snow White. Is this a poison apple Mom? Don't be silly her mother told her. So she ate it anyway.

The girl rode in a little boat that went around a pool and rang the bell in a small fire engine while waving to her parents. She had golden sea foam candy that melted to a hard little nugget of sweet sugar on her tongue. The best part of all was the small Ferris wheel. Are you sure you can go on by yourself? her mother asked. The girl nodded so excited she jumped up and down at least three times. Don't move around in the seat her mother told her.

The wheel stopped at the top and she could see the entire fair. She could see Borden Park where they went to the wading pool once. She could see the pictures of other families double exposed with hers. A mother a father one two kids holding hands holding bouffant pink cotton candy holding shiny red candy apples holding on.

She saw her parents standing on the pavement below. In this picture her mother would be caught looking up at her father with her mouth shaping a word the beginning of a question. Her hand would be on his shoulder and he would be puffing on a lit cigarette in his mouth getting the end of it red hot enough to light a cigarette for her. Maybe the word would be the date in small black letters at the bottom of the picture. They looked up at the girl smiling shielding their eyes from the flash of the sun. Everything was alright.

When the ride was over the carny unlocked the safety bar and she ran to her parents and hugged them both. We're not going yet are we? she said. We'll stay a little while longer her mother said. Her father threw his cigarette to the ground and sparks of red fell away from the butt.

The sky was turning an orange red and there was noise from the rides and people laughing and music coming from somewhere and they walked along an asphalt path created by booths and trailers and souvenir kiosks and ticket sales tables for dream homes gold bricks and the chance for just plain money and then there was a huge painted sign. A fresco a mural a false front on what was really just a big trailer. THE SMALLEST HORSE IN THE WORLD THE SMALLEST MAN IN THE WORLD THE BEARDED LADY. The metal sound of a man's voice blared across a loud speaker urging them to come inside that the price of admission was well worth it.

Should we go in? the girl's mother said. No I'm not too keen on it her father said. We might as well go while we're here we don't want to miss anything. So the girl's father paid the money and they went in. The passageway was narrow and the dirty-carpet-covered floor creaked. The girl was very quiet. There it was. The small horse in a small glass-fronted cage. The smell was heavy sharp with manure and urine and it stung her nostrils like the smell of the barn on her grandparents' farm. Straw was strewn on the floor and there was a fresh turd sitting like an insult by the horse's back hooves. Its hooves were no bigger than her hands and curled upward. It just stood there looking straight ahead at nothing. It blinked through a light brown fringe that hid its sad eyes. Can we ask to take the horse home Mom? the girl said. Don't be silly where would we keep it? Besides it's foundered her mother said. The world's smallest man was dressed like a gladiator. He had large hands and sat on a small three-legged stool in the corner of the room with a bottle of Coca-Cola in his hand. He didn't look happy either so the girl smiled at him. He met her eyes then quickly looked away and took a drink from his bottle of Coke.

When the girl saw the bearded lady she was appalled and fascinated at the same time. The woman was framed in her glass fronted cage dressed in a long shimmering low cut blue dress and had shiny brown back-combed hair turned up in a flip. There were trickles of sweat on her forehead. She really did have a beard after all. It was lighter than the woman's hair and was shaped into a point that fell to her collarbone. I think it's really a man the girl's mother said. The girl didn't think so. She wondered what the bearded lady did all day and whether she was allowed to go to the bathroom. Why didn't she just shave off her beard? the girl thought. Sure she wouldn't be the bearded lady just a lady but maybe she could sing songs or tell jokes or become an acrobat. If she shaved off her beard then she wouldn't have to worry when she did tricks about getting tangled in her beard and having an accident. She wanted to tell her if she shaved off her beard it would be alright.

Outside the air was cooling the sun had turned into a red disk that took up most of the sky. The pavement was still hot and the girl's legs and feet were beginning to ache. Let me win you something her father said to her mother. No we can't afford it she said. C'mon let's just go take a look and he kissed her cheek and put his arm around her waist leading them down a path with booths on either side. Stuffed plush animals hung off the roofs of the stalls carnies stood outside pointing to people walking by. How 'bout it mister? Win a little something for the wife? Her father tried to toss quarters onto plates but they just bounced off. Don't you know there are springs under those plates? her mother said. It's just for fun her father said and tried to toss a basketball into an apple basket. The basket is smaller than the ball it's just a waste of money her mother said.

Finally he got to a booth with milk bottles lined up in a row across a back shelf. Huge teddy bears hung enticingly from the rafters. C'mon mister give 'er a try. The carny tossed him the ball. The girl's father laughed and tossed it at the middle bottle. A miss. He tossed another. Missed again. He paid for ball after ball and tossed again and again. Can I try Dad? the girl asked. No I'll do it he said. Let's go we won't have any money left her mother said. The girl's father already had the next ball raised past his right shoulder. He kept on throwing. He kept on throwing trying to win the girl's mother another one of the big smiling teddy bears he kept on throwing until he was out of money. Nothing left and nothing to show for it. Her mother held her little sister who had fallen asleep on her shoulder. Are we going? the girl asked her parents. Yes her mother said. Her father walked ahead of them through the noise and the smell of popcorn cotton candy tiny donuts. The darkening sky. His head down smoking a cigarette. The girl felt a lot of time had passed.

Her father started the car and lit a cigarette from the lighter in the car. The girl could feel the heat from the lighter all the way in the back seat. They drove home with the windows down. Her sister slept. Her father turned on the radio and blew smoke against the windshield. Her mother stared out the window. Do I have to have a bath tonight? the girl asked. No just wash your feet in the tub.

‹›‹›‹›

It was getting dark outside. The bathroom was lit by the bulb above the mirror. The small room was shadow and contrast. Her mother stood in front of the mirror and covered the girl in shadow as she sat on the side of the bathtub. In this tiny room the hollow sound of tepid water swishing in the tub echoed like an explosion. I wish Dad could've won a bear hey Mom?

Her mother reached under the sink for the wire brush rollers and white plastic picks she kept in a bread bag. Dropped the bag into the sink. Not this time I guess she said.

Her mother was inside the camera. The photograph waiting to be taken. Shiny black hair short white sleeveless nightgown. She took a black comb and used the tail to mark out a square boundary of hair from her forehead for the first roller. She pulled the piece straight up and the girl felt the pull on her own scalp. Her mother quickly swivelled the roller until all the hair had disappeared around it and then pierced it with a white pick. When she was done her head was subdivided into segments bordered in narrow white lines. She put the empty bread bag under the sink.

The girl dried her feet with a threadbare towel while her mother sat beside her on the side of the tub cupping a small black and white striped beanbag ashtray in the palm of her left hand and scissoring a cigarette between the index and middle finger of her right hand. The water emptied from the tub the last bit rushing down the drain with a slurp and leaving behind a narrow trail of sand.

You had a lot of sweets today I hope you're not going to be sick her mother said. Sweet sea foam candy the girl said and smiled at her mother who tried to smile back. Where did this sand come from? C'mon get to bed she said but did not get up from the side of the tub. The two of them sat in the small bathroom the toilet tank seeming to exhale as water trickled for a moment the light bulb was the faintest of sounds the hardwood under their feet creaked. The cigarette slowly burned to nothing between her mother's fingers. Her mother's black hair tightly contained on a head-full of curlers the inside of the white bathtub now filled with their shadows. Sweet sea foam candy the girl said softly. Her mother opened the taps full on and then off and hurried the last few grains of sand to the drain.

‹›‹›‹›

Thin hardsand crust on the beach after a rain.
The sand breaking away from her feet in the shapes
of geometry as she ran. One day soon she and her
sister would learn to swim in the lake. Floating on
their backs and paddling in shallow water around
their mother's legs. Her mother turning in circles to
watch them making sure they stayed afloat watching
for any change in the waves in breathing in depth
of water in depth of field. Where was her father?
She couldn't see him but she felt sure he would be
there sitting on shore smoking cigarettes and looking
out at them as they swam.

Sand sweet as sea foam candy sticking to her feet when
she finally got out of the water. She hoped she'd never
forget how to swim.

2

There were 13 white balloons leftover from her birthday weeks ago.
Can you blow them all up Mom? the girl said.
I'm not blowing up 13 balloons it's unlucky.
Then could you blow up three balloons?
Three? Yes I can blow up three.
The girl had taken them out of the plastic bag and laid each one on the table. Stick. Circle. Stick. Circle. And the girl's mother stretched the flat balloons this way and that. Breathing life into each and twisting the ends around her finger and quickly into knots.
Now I want you to take it easy today her mother said. Her stomach hurt this Tuesday morning. Too much sun yesterday her mother said and had given her two teaspoons of Dr. Fowler's Strawberry Extract. Her mother kept the strawberry extract in the medicine cabinet and the girl liked to open the cabinet door and just look at it sometimes. This clear beautiful red in a glass bottle. She did not think it tasted anything like strawberries though. It was bitter. It stung her throat and stayed on her tongue like a lie.

The girl held the three balloons in her arms. She moved slowly toward the veranda. Opened her arms and the balloons fell lazily to the floor. Two eyes and a mouth straight across.

She picked up one of the sticks and rubbed it against her hair. Stuck the balloon against the wall. The shadow of the white balloon on the white wall. A grey sliver. She picked up a round balloon and rubbed it against her hair. Stuck it to the wall under the first.

She was learning to read and learning to write. An ! meant excited.

The girl sat cross-legged on the veranda floor and imagined she was floating on the wide planks of worn pale grey. A colouring book rested in front of her and she dumped her box of crayons on the floor. The paper had to be peeled back on some of the crayons. Red. Orange. Yellow. She picked up the narrow sticks held them in her fist and considered. Flames. Leaves in fall. The colours in the windows of the church across the street.

She picked at the yellow paper covering the crayon. Peeled it away and underneath was clean pure yellow. Not like the tip of the yellow crayon speckled with tiny dots of the darker crayons navy blue, brown, green.

The sun was still behind the house and at the front in the veranda it was cool and the light shining through the windows was pale and reasonable. She noticed some sand stuck between her toes and brushed it away. Her shoulders hurt. She had gotten a sunburn yesterday at the lake. Her mother had put cold Noxzema on her shoulders. It had helped a bit but her skin sent heat right through the white coating. The burn had been worth it because she had learned to swim yesterday.

It was a summer long weekend and they were up early this Monday morning. Her Dad wasn't going to work today and they were going to the lake. The sun was already starting to get hot and it was still early in the morning.

The girl got into her red bathing suit right after breakfast. She was careful not to eat too much puffed wheat because her mother had told her if you eat right before you swim you could get cramps and drown.
What are cramps? she had asked.
Pains you in your stomach your legs arms her mother said.
But you don't swim with your stomach do you?
Doesn't matter. You could get a stomach cramp double over and sink to the bottom of the lake. And you don't want to get caught in the weeds either her mother said. You could get tangled up and pulled under. As her mother told her this fact she twisted her tea towel-wrapped fist in a yellow Melmac cup and put it in the cupboard.
Her mother's movements were quick and constant. Drying dishes folding towels lighting and smoking a cigarette her hands never stopped.

Her father came into the kitchen wearing one of his short-sleeved plaid work shirts and navy blue swim trunks that stopped just above his knees. He cradled a rolled up towel under his arm.
Ready to hit the road? he asked. The girl so rarely saw her father wear anything other than his work clothes. He looked out of place standing in the kitchen with bare legs and bare feet.
Just about. Run and get a towel he told the girl.
The girl opened the door of the closet. The mismatched faded towels were neatly folded twice into each other. Folds facing out so that the stacks looked like squished Cs waiting to escape and fly out to make words. *Cat-cap-cup.* She took a towel and held it like a baby.

On the kitchen table her mother spread Cheez Whiz on slices of bread stacked them on top of a piece of wax paper. Quickly folding and tucking and the layers of white and orange were covered in an opaque crackle now quiet. She wrapped peanut butter cookies like she was rolling pennies. The sandwiches cookies and a Tupperware pitcher of Kool-Aid went into a big brown paper bag.
What are you taking to drink? the girl's father asked.
Kool-Aid.
No pop?
Pop doesn't quench your thirst.
Well I want a pop.
Can we have pop too Mom? the girl asked.

Look what you started the girl's mother said. Why can't you just have what everybody else is having? Why do I have to listen to you all the time? Wait for you in the car he said. She heard three thuds as he knocked his work boots together.
What are you wearing on your feet? she asked him.
Work boots.
You can't wear work boots to the lake she said.
Only thing I got—I'm not wearing my good shoes. These'll be fine. I'll take them off when I get there.

The girl's mother shook her head almost imperceptibly sighed closed her eyes and under her breath the girl thought she heard her ask to no one why she even bothered. She bunched the top of the paper bag closed and called for the girl to hurry up the best part of the day will be gone. Held the door for her two kids and locked it once they were on the porch stairs.

Their '65 Ford Galaxie was parked on the two ruts running straight from the back alley to their backyard. The father was sitting in the driver's seat.

Watch your fingers the girl's mother said. The doors slammed in the heat. The girl and her sister sat in the backseat and their father started the car backing into the alley stretching his arm across the back of the seat as he looked out the back window. His hand touched his wife's shoulder and without looking at him she flicked his hand away. He stopped in the alley and patted his shirt pocket taking out his package of cigarettes.

Gotta stop for smokes he said and drove up to the corner to wait for a break in traffic on the main road.

The girl was fascinated by two buildings in her neighbourhood.

The church across the street though she had never actually been inside It's not our church her mother said. Their church was small and white and smelled soft of wood incense candles and furnace. Her father didn't come to church with them. It wasn't his church he said. The corner grocery store seemed faraway and just as out of reach. Her mother told her she wasn't allowed to go to either alone. Ever.

He gunned it across 66th Street and parked at the side of the grey shingle-covered two-storey Santa Rosa Grocery Store. He left the car running and the radio on. Nancy Wilson sang: "... and youdon'tknowyou don'tknowyoudon'tknowyoudon'tknow ... how glad I am ..." How much longer will he be? the girl thought. She wanted to get to the lake so badly. There he was. Throwing open the store's screen door his shirtfront blowing open just slightly his legs pale sticking out of his work boots.

Back behind the wheel he put a paper bag on the front seat between him and his wife. Pushed in the cigarette lighter.
What did you get Dad? The girl peeked over the seat to look inside the bag. A bottle of cream soda and a Cuban Lunch chocolate bar.
Did you get us a pop Dad? the girl asked.
He didn't answer.
Dad?
Never mind he said. Her mother tsked. The lighter popped out and her father put the red-hot circle to the end of his cigarette puffing hard until the tip of the cigarette burned red against the blue through the windshield. Smoke filled the front of the car and made the back feel even hotter.

Her father drove around the block and turned on to 118th Avenue. Past the brick Safeway past the three brick buildings she thought so beautiful the brick furniture store with the big sign over the front door shaped like a **!** that at night was neon-lit with green and blue. Past the second hand stores the Tastee-Freez and the Beverly Crest hotel. Past the dump just outside the city where a bulldozer pushed piles of garbage and gulls flew down and up.
What a stink! the girl said.
Try not to breathe her mother said. The girl held her breath until they got over the Clover Bar bridge until her face got even hotter and her heart beat fast and her

parents just kept looking straight ahead at the highway and off into the sky. She let out her breath. She didn't want to die of suffocation. She breathed in and out and held her breath again when they passed by the plastics factory. After that she didn't have to hold her breath. It was highway and farmland and the same road they always took when they went back to Saskatchewan to visit her mother's family. Except her parents weren't talking this trip. Her sister had fallen asleep beside her and it was just the music on the radio and the highway wind rumbling through the open windows. Her parents smoking and staring straight ahead.

Watch for the wire fence you might see a buffalo her mother said. So the girl sat up straight and looked out the window.

They turned into Elk Island Park and stopped at the little house. Her father got a sticker and got out of the car to stick it to the outside of the windshield. They drove on through the hot day the trees speckling dark shadows on the road. She could smell the lake. They parked the car. Her mother woke her sister up and she cried her hair stuck to her forehead. The girl was so excited. Can we run to the lake Mom? No stay right by me her mother said.

Her father's work boots crunched the gravel in the parking lot. The girl could feel the rocks through the thin rubber of her bright blue flip-flops which were already imprinted with the shape of her steps. Her mother walked quickly over the rocks in her bare feet. The air smelled of cool lake. There were other families on the beach but they seemed small and her family seemed great and wonderful the four of them together with the lake so real not just a picture of water she might draw with her crayons. The hot sand and the lake and the trees and the bright clear sky made the moment seem even more wonderful. She tried to skip and her flip-flops flicked the hot sand back on her ankles.

Her mother carried her little sister and the bag of food. The pitcher of Kool-Aid had leaked a bit and one corner of the bag was wet. Her father followed carrying the paper bag with his pop and chocolate bar. His work boots kicked up sand behind him and left tracks that anyone could follow if they'd wanted to.
Here let's put the stuff here her father said when they came to a picnic table under a tree. It's pretty far from the water her mother said.
Not that far I'll stay and watch the food.
You're not coming in? her mother said.
I don't want to get water in my ears.
Just swim on top then her mother said in an irritated voice. Her father lit a cigarette.
Let's go in the lake Mom! and the girl grabbed her

mother's hand and pulled her toward the water. She didn't glance back at her father as she carried her little sister toward the lake. They stood in the wet seafoam sand algae lolling at their feet. Can I get tangled in these weeds Mom? the girl asked. The girl imagined fingers of seaweed circling her ankles and pulling her under.
No not these ones only in the deep parts of lakes. We're just going to stay near the shore. You need to respect the water. It's dangerous.
Teach me to swim then Mom.
Okay let's just walk out a ways. The water cooled the girl's skin. Green and cool and soothing with the belief that nothing could ever go wrong. Calm with the sound of the soft waves coming into shore.
Try floating on your back first and stay right by my legs where I can see you her mother said. She cupped water with her hand and scooped it over her sister's legs and arms. The little girl gasped at first at the cold and then laughed.

The girl sat on the lake bottom with her head above the water the sun warm against her face and her wet hair. She let the water lift her arms away from her side and opened her fingers her hands just beneath the water's surface. Her body felt cool and still but with a floor of sand under her she felt powerful against the size of the lake.

Okay now lift yourself up her mother said.
Hold my hand the girl said to her mother. Her mother bent over and held her hand.
Kick your feet and move your hand side to side.
The girl did as she was told and sank under the water going up her nose. She stood coughing and sneezed the lake water out her nose.
Try again her mother said. She sat on the bottom of the lake again her head above the water. Lifted off and kicked her legs.
Hold your breath so you don't get water up your nose her mother said. The girl kicked her legs and moved her hand with a quick sculling motion on just one side. She did this again and again for what seemed like a very long time. Her mother held her hand and the girl's younger sister was quite happy to look down at the girl suspended above the water in the crook of her mother's free arm.

Again the girl kicked her feet. Again she sculled quickly back and forth. Where was her father? The girl felt as if she were on top of the water. Felt it was holding her up and she was floating.
Let go of my hand she said to her mother. She kicked and sculled now with both hands.
Keep kicking her mother said. And off she went. I'm swimming! She yelled and her mother laughed and her sister laughed and kicked her legs too. Dad I'm swimming she shouted and she tried to turn her head

toward the table but couldn't see him. Where was her father? She swam and swam until her legs and arms were so tired.

I don't want to forget how to swim the girl said.

You won't her mother told her. It's one of those things that's just like second nature. Like riding a bike. C'mon let's eat our lunch. And they walked from the water through the hard sea foam sand and up to the table under the tree. Her father was sitting in the shade the laces of his work boots loosened so the tongues almost touched the sand.

Did you see me swim Dad?

Yep sure did. Pretty good there. Her mother didn't look at her father as they sat and ate Cheez Whiz sandwiches that were warm but the girl convinced herself they were like grilled cheese. Can I go back in Mom? the girl asked. Wait half an hour her mother said so you don't get a cramp. The girl looked out at the water at the waves coming toward her with the same rhythm each time like the cars that pass on the highway whoosh whoosh like the cars and trucks she heard passing by so fast back and forth along 66th Street past the Santa Rosa Grocery Store. And her father asked if she wanted to share some cream soda or some Cuban Lunch and as much as she wanted to taste the beautiful pink pop and the chocolate because it was one of her favourites she said no because she wanted to swim some more to make sure she hadn't forgotten how to swim and she didn't want to get a cramp. So her father drank the pop and ate all the chocolate because her mother had already told him: You should know by now I don't like sweets and pop doesn't quench my thirst.

The girl ran from the shade to the edge of the water. Don't you dare go in her mother called and the girl asked could she go in to her ankles. No you don't go in without me. So the girl stood just out of reach of the wave and looked at the impression her feet left in the sand. Her mother made the same shapes in the steamed-up car windows in winter. Pressed the side of her fist to the glass and used her index finger to make five toes on top. The girl remembered them both laughing once at the tiny footprints climbing up the steamy window. The girl glanced back at her parents sitting in the shade smoking cigarettes. They both looked angry but they were saying nothing.
Her mother finished her cigarette and said to her father: If you want to be miserable for the sake of being miserable go right ahead. She took the girls back into the water.
Come and swim Dad the girl called. But her father smiled and said he had to stay at the table to make sure ants and flies didn't get the food.
The girl paddled around her mother over and over and asked could they go out a little deeper? Just a bit and she took about three steps back from the shore. The girl stood up and the water was to her chest. She lifted off

the sandy bottom and kept on paddling and sculling. She swam and swam until her legs felt weak and rubbery and her mother said it was time to go home because everyone was tired.
I'm not tired the girl said. Well you will be her mother said. They walked to the car with the sun started to hit the tips of the tallest trees around the lake and when they passed a garbage bin her father threw away the bag.

The girl sat on her damp towel on the way home. The bottom of her flip-flops were coated with sand and she could feel a scratching between her toes. She dangled her flip-flops from her toes. She was beginning to feel a bit cold.

Her parents sat in the front seat and her mother was out of her kind of cigarettes so she said she'd bum one from her Dad. And when she took the first puff said how can you smoke these things? And he said it's better than the burning cough drops she smoked.

The girl looked hard for buffalo but didn't see any. The girl didn't even say how much the factory and the dump stunk. She held her breath without anyone noticing.

The house was cool when they got home. The kitchen table with its thick chrome legs chrome trim and grey speckled top had a few cookie crumbs on it and the Cheez Whiz smeared on the knife in the sink had turned hard.

A quick bath and then to bed her mother said. The girl heard the sound of the TV muffled over the sound of the water running in the bathtub.

As she lay in bed that night she felt happy that she had learned to swim today. It was as if she was now part of a big secret world. This was a secret place that didn't exist for people who just walked around everyday on sidewalks and drove on the road and parked in ruts in a backyard. This secret place went farther than the grocery store and farther than the church.

She heard laughter coming from the TV. It made her feel safe and so she slept.

Now here she was Tuesday morning on the veranda with the leftover balloons from her birthday her crayons and colouring book. Her shoulders would hurt from sunburn for a few days her mother said. Keep busy it'll take your mind off it she told the girl. The phone rang. Okay you can stay out here and play her mother said. And she heard her mother say well hello stranger and she knew it was her grandmother by the tone in her mother's voice she was so happy.

So the girl coloured the sky red on this page the sun was going to set and she coloured the tree red because the light was shining on it. And the colour made her think of the cream soda her father had offered her yesterday that she hadn't taken because she'd been afraid. Maybe she could go to the store and get some herself. Maybe she could get a Cuban Lunch after all and maybe something for her mother. Maybe just gum.

She put on her flip-flops and walked quietly and quickly to her room pressing her toes together so the flip-flops wouldn't slap against her feet and make a noise. She opened up the top drawer of her dresser. It had a nick in the top right corner and the shiny gold handle that looked like a **U** was loose. She reached underneath the short-sleeved cotton blouses her mother had folded so neatly and retrieved a white envelope with her name on the outside. Pulled out the card Happy Birthday and opened it. Inside was a $2 bill her grandmother had sent her. She squeezed it in her fist and put the envelope back in the drawer. Walked past her mother steadying the phone in the crook of her neck while she did dishes her back to the girl. Yes she got the two dollars thanks Mom the girl heard her mother say.

This wasn't lying it was just a little secret and she didn't always have to listen to her mother did she? She was older now and she had learned how to swim. Through the veranda and out the front door open the gate of twisted wire. She could see the store just across 66th Street. It wasn't so far really. She really felt she had missed out on the cream soda and chocolate bar. She clutched the $2 and ran past her backyard past the alley past the neighbour's house. She got to the corner and heard the loud sound of cars and trucks rumbling both ways on the busy street.

3

The name of the neighbourhood was a saint's name: Santa Rosa. Her friend who lived across the alley said well Saint Rose was a real saint after all and this Sunday was her day. Every saint had its day and this Sunday was hers. A saint right in the neighbourhood with a name that told her story.

She liked roses and hurting herself the girl's friend told her.

Hurting herself?

Yeah like hitting herself and punishing herself.

Didn't her Mom and Dad do that? the girl asked.

No she did it on her own I think.

What do you do on her feast day? Would Saint Rose visit the neighbourhood? the girl asked.

No she's been dead a long time now her friend said way more than 10 years but you can still pray to her and she might even answer you. Candles help.

But the girl wasn't allowed to light matches.

Will Saint Rose answer you even if you don't light a candle? the girl asked her friend.

Probably not. Candles mean you're trying harder so she'll pay more attention.

The girl thought there seemed to be more praying and more chances to dress up in her friend's church. Her friend's church was the biggest building in the neighbourhood. Bigger than the grocery store more beautiful and more mysterious. Its windows had pictures she couldn't quite make out but she could see the colours on the glass all her very favourites from her box of crayons.

The girl thought about the time her friend wore a long white lace dress and a white veil held on her head with a circle of tiny white roses. Her friend wore white gloves and shiny white shoes and looked very serious but happy at the same time.

It was spring. Sunday morning and the light was still soft. Quiet. The girl's friend was walking to church with her Mom and Dad and her five brothers and sisters. Her friend's whole family walked along together on the sidewalk in the sun shining at the side of the girl's house on that Sunday morning.

The girl sat on the concrete step at the bottom of the back porch. The step was cold and rough. She had her skirt wrapped around her knees the folds of thick cotton with its busy geometric shapes circles dashes. The girl trying to squeeze the cold shapes from the fabric hugging the skirt to her knees and feeling every stitch on the arms of the red sweater her mother had knit her. Long raised rows along her arms.

The last small pile of dirty snow behind the back porch on this side of the house had melted but she was sure she could still taste snow in the air knowing it was just under the mottled green and still brown winter remnants of grass. She was sure the cold shade on the far side of the house was still holding on to the colour and taste of winter but she wanted winter gone.

The girl could see her friend's family through the narrow twisted white wire of the fence wound like fingers between the white fence posts. It was as if the family moved in slow motion. All of them in their best clothes the mother in a pale green dress and the girls in the palest pink yellow blue and wearing sweaters the colour of cream. The father and the two boys wore grey suits and white shirts and blue red grey striped ties.

While the rest of her friend's family faded into grey and the outline of their bodies softened then dissolved into the colour of the asphalt on the street a bright light seemed to shine only on her friend who looked to the girl like an angel a dream-ghost in white.

The girl ran into the backyard to break off some branches from the big tree. A gift for her friend. Soft grey furry buds jutted like tiny rabbit's feet from the branches. When she ran back to give them to her friend the toe of her shoe caught on a crack in the sidewalk and she fell hard on her knees with the sticks still in her hand. She didn't cry she didn't say anything either just handed the branches to her friend over the fence and ran into the house. Her knees were scraped badly and bleeding. The knuckles on her right hand were scratched.

The girl sat on the side of the bathtub while her mother tried to wipe away the small specks of sand and dirt.

Her mother took red Mercurochrome down from the medicine cabinet shelf. Red liquid in a small glass bottle. Attached to its golden bottle top was a thin wire wand with a small round sponge at the end. Soaked with red. The mother rubbed the sponge in a circular motion on the girl's knees to kill the germs. The girl didn't know whether it hurt more to bend her knees or straighten them. She could feel the cool air on her knees. The girl sat for a moment watching the red sink into her skin. Her knees looked like her mother had sewn on big red buttons.

When you don't cry I always know you're really hurt the girl's mother said.

The girl was proud she didn't cry even though her knees seemed to be spreading the red hurt over her whole body.

The girl and her mother had watched a black and white movie called *The Song of Bernadette*. Bernadette was a saint too but not in this neighbourhood. She was a saint in France who had a lot of pain in her leg but she discovered a spring that cured her and also cured a lot of other people. Bernadette saw things and heard voices but some people didn't believe her. In the movie Bernadette is in a lot of pain. But she still seems happy in some parts.

The girl and her mother watched another black and white movie about another saint:

Joan of Arc. She's a very famous saint the girl's mother said. She wasn't a saint from the neighbourhood either. The girl thought Joan of Arc seemed very energetic and knew her mind just like Nancy Drew. Joan of Arc saw things and heard voices like Saint Bernadette. By the end of the movie people had stopped liking Joan of Arc and called her a witch.

What happened to Joan of Arc? the girl asked her mother who was trying to nap on the couch while one child beside her the other asleep in her crib. She answered the girl without opening her eyes. Burnt at the stake her mother said.
In the movie Joan of Arc was very brave. She was just coughing a little bit at the end when puffs of smoke started to rise to the top of the screen. All you could see was Joan of Arc's face and then the light faded from the edges of the screen to a pinhole and then the screen went all dark. When was Joan of Arc's day?

So tomorrow was Saint Rose's feast day and the girl was excited. It was something exciting to happen in the neighbourhood and her friend's church was just across the street from her so she might be able to see the feast.

The church was one of the two big buildings in her neighbourhood. The other was the Santa Rosa Grocery which she had been inside before and tried to sneak to by herself but she had never been inside her friend's church. When the girl looked out the veranda window she could see the big church's steps through the branches of a tall dark green pine. The church steps went on for a long time so many and so high she could not see the church door from the veranda window. The fence around the building was brown brick the same colour of brown brick as the church. It would be hard for her to sneak across the street up all those stairs and into the church by herself. Anyway she had been told never to sneak away on her own again ever so she thought she probably wouldn't try it. Her mother was keeping a close watch on her now and there was probably somebody at the church watching her as well. Maybe the ghost of Saint Rose on her feast day. Maybe even God.

So tomorrow it's Saint Rose's feast day the girl told her mother at the kitchen table. The late morning light was soft because the window faced west. Her mother was drinking coffee from a pink Melmac cup the light a thin veneer on her dark hair her arm her wrist her hands. You'll have a head start then the girl's mother said.

Her grandmother was going to take her on the bus and they would do some shopping and then eat at the luncheonette.

The girl's mother had slept with rollers in her hair the night before so this morning she sat at the table with her hair puffy and curled up at the ends. The girl was a bit tired after a rough sleep. It was hard to get comfortable in prickly brush rollers. Her mother just couldn't stand it when her hair hung in her face so she had clipped two red plastic barrettes on each side of her head. The girl's hair looked like curtains opening on a window.

She watched for her grandmother to get off at the bus stop on 66th Street saw her on the sidewalk waiting to cross when the bus drove away and then there she was knocking softly on the back screen door. The girl's mother opened the door and it made a short quick squeak. Come in. Hello. Hi. The girl's mother and grandmother did not use each other's name.

Don't you look smart the grandmother said to the girl. The girl felt smart too and had washed her face brushed her teeth and put on her good dress.
Are things a bit better? The grandmother asked the girl's mother. The girl didn't know things were worse. Better or worse.
I s'pose so her mother said.
You'll have to get back to how you were when you were courting she said. The girl's mother lit a cigarette.
I don't know the girl's mother said and tsked the way she sometimes did when she was sad or disappointed or surprised.
You'll make the best of things she said to her daughter-in-law. Everything will work out alright.

The girl's grandmother seemed to remember suddenly that the girl was standing right beside her. We'd better go before all the best things get bought up her grandmother said and smiled at her.

The girl's mother gave her a hug and kiss and said Be good. Her grandmother held her hand as they crossed 66th Street. Her grandmother always wore her soft beige gloves and her beige chiffon scarf when she went downtown and though the girl's grandmother had told her she looked smart the girl wished she was as fancy and dressed up.

Their bus came and they both got on her grandmother dropping the exact change in the glass box and it clanked to the bottom. She got a transfer for herself but the girl rode for free. The girl sat by the window feeling important and at the beginning of something special. The bus started and stopped people got on and off along 118th Avenue past the music shop the furniture store bakery and clinic around the traffic circle and past the store her mother went to for fabric. Then they were there.

Pull the string her grandmother told her. It rang and red letters lit up at the front of the bus. They got off in front of the Strand Theatre.

We've got time to kill before lunch her grandmother said. They went into the Hudson's Bay Store. Music played in the background. Violins. But from the record

department the girl could hear the Dave Clark Five
and she and her grandmother walked the smooth
wood floors past the make-up counter the shiny shoes
and the scarves. Folded silk and colours fanned on the
counter like cards pick a card pick a scarf.
Her grandmother took off her gloves and picked up
a paisley scarf green brown orange thick heavy silk.
She tied it around her neck and looked in the round
mirror on the counter.
It's beautiful the girl said.
I'll take this her grandmother said to the clerk.
You can pay right over there ma'am the clerk said.
Her grandmother carried the scarf to the cash like
an offering.
I don't want anyone thinking I'm going to steal this
she whispered to the girl. There's always someone
watching you in these stores. Don't think there isn't.
The girl wondered if Saint Rose and maybe God were
watching her in the Hudson's Bay Store too. She might
need to believe in that.

At the cash her grandmother handed over a bill and
searched for change.
I have some silver and copper in here and she flicked
around the coins in the zippered compartment of her
black leather wallet with her index finger. The clerk
put the change into the correct cash compartments
and the bill face up under the clip.
The two were out the door her grandmother stopping
to put on her gloves.

Should we make our way to the café? It's close enough
to lunch. Are you hungry?
Sure am the girl said and smiled at her grandmother
who she thought so elegant and glamourous and smart.
Walking down Jasper Avenue and left to Kresge's.
The girl loved this place. The entrance was round and
the letters rested on smooth shiny stone. She imagined
running her hand slowly over the windows and cool
stone above the doors tracing each letter with her finger.
Narrow letters K R E S G E ' S.
The glass doors shone and her grandmother held the
right one open for her as the girl passed under her arm.
She could smell her grandmother's perfume a trace of
flowers. The girl stopped just inside the doors.

The luncheonette.
Red and white tile floors like teeth or piano keys from
a piano and the keys could be any colour she chose.
The music would be hers and would taste the colour
of the keys. The sound: the colour. Would red keys
really make the music sound different? She could taste
each letter their sound their music.

And there was an endless long counter shiny brown
and edged with chrome and a line of red and silver
chairs like buttons sewn to their metal posts and pinned
to the red and white tile floors. The tiles jutted like
teeth toward the luncheonette counter the floor one
silent mouth ready to close on the golden yellow

Melmac dishes the signs advertising Hot BEEF Sandwich Delicious CHICKEN Dinner. The old-fashioned stove a cooler milkshake makers a deep fryer and huge toaster. The teeth on the floor were waiting to close their mouth around the people on the chairs.

The luncheonette reminded her of church and she felt the same sense of occasion when she sat on the smooth shiny red button of her seat as she felt when she sat in the smooth wooden pews at church.

So happy. Her grandmother took off her gloves and stacked them on the counter. She untied her scarf and put it in her purse. Snap shut and then laid on her lap. The girl could smell her hand lotion like roses. Her face was smooth with powder and there were just a few lines around her eyes.

Afternoon ladies the waitress said. What can I get for you?
I'll have a hot dog with ketchup and a small Pepsi the girl said loudly. Please her grandmother whispered. Please.
I'll have the hot chicken sandwich and a coffee please the grandmother said.
Coming right up. The waitress scribbled on a yellow pad with blue lines and moved quickly to someone else who had just sat down at the end of the long counter.
You are getting so big the girl's grandmother said. Here let's take off that jacket so you don't get over-heated.

I don't want you catching a cold.
The girl draped her sweater over the back of the chair. Chrome back bones.
This is a nice little treat for us then the girl's grandmother said and the girl told her about it being St. Rose's feast day in the neighbourhood tomorrow and how she hoped her mother was going to make a lot for them to eat.

The girl thought about her mother and grandmother talking nervously at the back door. She felt grown up sitting there on the red button chair and wanted to say something important. So she told her grandmother about the argument her parents had and how their voices were so loud they woke her up then she laughed when she said this because that's just what grown-ups did when they told a story. Her mother had laughed before when the girl asked her about her mother and father shouting at each other. Oh it was just a silly argument she would say. It's alright. Don't worry so much. The girl wanted to tell her grandmother about how she just lay on her bed in the dark afraid to move her parents' voices making her feel like she didn't know what to do. These weren't the same as the voices Joan of Arc or St. Bernadette heard only in their heads these were real voices. The girl didn't know if she should pretend she didn't hear them or get out of bed and ask her parents what was wrong. But she didn't want to get out of bed to look down the hall in case she saw ghosts. Shadows of her parents and the shadows of their voices. Their voices floated toward her face like the smoke in the Joan of Arc movie. Maybe she was scared she'd see the ghost of St. Bernadette walking quietly through the house. Scared St. Bernadette would be able to sneak up on her parents and hear what they were saying and know what they shouted at each other for and had arguments that seemed more scary than silly. The girl thought she might want to know but was scared of what St. Bernadette might tell her. It might be something she shouldn't know after all. But the girl said none of that. She waited for her grandmother to laugh along but she didn't.

The waitress brought the Pepsi in a big clear glass that bubbled and frothed with ice and a bent straw with red stripes that tried to hide itself inside the glass. Her grandmother still said nothing when her coffee came. She took a white paper serviette from the chrome dispenser and set it on top of the saucer then placed the cup in the depression left. The girl's grandmother flicked at the counter but the girl couldn't see a crumb or anything to be worried about brushing away.

The waitress brought the food and thin white ribbons of vapour floated off her grandmother's plate. The girl started to eat the hot dog from the middle out. There's too much bread for me she told her grandmother and her grandmother smiled and cut her own sandwich into small pieces and didn't drip any gravy on herself at all.

This is an early feast for us right Gramma? the girl said.
It sure is she said. I think your eyes were bigger than your stomach this time. Can you eat all that?
I don't think I can I want to leave some room for a sundae. Could I have a strawberry sundae Gramma?
Yes you sure can. Just leave what you can't eat. Wipe your mouth you have some ketchup there.
She wiped her mouth hard with a scratchy serviette.
I'm done she told her grandmother. There were still two pieces of hot dog bun on her white plate but the girl couldn't wait to order a sundae.
The grandmother flicked at the counter again.

The girl saw the waitresses in their clean pressed red uniforms rushing from person to person place to place and the music in the background was Ferry Cross the Mersey and she thought it was mercy and she hoped things would be alright. She looked down the counter at the faces with their features all lined up the way people looked kneeling in the in the pews at church their hands clasped in front of them like they were waiting for their order to come up.

She just felt so lucky and special to be at the luncheonette all dressed up and feeling full of hot dog and pop and all the noise of milkshakes being made and knives and forks on the counter and the waitress laughing with the customers and saying right away hold your horses but not in a mean way. This was the best way to spend the Saturday before Saint Rose's feast day. This was really a feast day the girl thought. There were even plastic red roses in the glass vase on the counter in front of them.

4

Men came to the girl's little pink house on the corner to try and sell things to her mother. Every time one of these men came to the pink house her mother would open the front door and stand square in the frame. Her feet planted far apart her one hand on the frame and the other gripping the door handle. Her mother was not a large woman but when she stood like that she had a strength the girl wanted to take in. Her mother's short curled and quickly-combed hair and her apron wrapped around her like armour and a damp dishtowel dangling from her right hand like some weapon made her think of Joan of Arc.

The sunlight shone pink and golden through the veranda's windows and between the spaces of her mother's body like the women on the church windows. So much singing! And when her mother opened the door it was as if she were rising to heaven light shining around her pale blue pants her white shirt her white slippers in the white frame of the front door of the little pink house. So much singing!

These men came to the door carrying leather cases like treasure chests and she thought that with their shiny shoes and their long coats and hats and faces with no whiskers the men looked like princes in the fairy tales, or a saint or maybe Jesus if he had shaved off his beard.

Sometimes her mother seemed to know what these men were going to say before they said it. They might touch the brim of their hat and that would be enough. Her mother would just say no thanks and slam the door. Sometimes her mother would say no without a thank you before she slammed the door and sometimes she said nothing. Just slammed the door and locked it.

Once there was a man who came to the door selling salves and ointments. *Salves* and *ointments*. Her mother told him he could come into the house but didn't take his coat only flicked the dishtowel in the direction of the kitchen table and told the man to go sit in there. The girl said *salves* and *ointments* over and over in her mind. As the man gently set his case on the floor beside the silver legs of the kitchen chair she thought *salves ointments.*

As he set little bottles full of different colours on the table and placed flat round tins in front of them she thought *salves ointments*. Shiny tins painted with gold and silver and red. The story of the three wise men. Gold. Frankincense. Myrrh. This man seemed wise. He put his navy blue hat gently on the table and the girl couldn't help but stare at it. There was a tiny red feather in the hat band and the man's long dark blue coat was folded on the back of the kitchen chair and it looked clean and new. The deep blue colour was like

her midnight blue crayon like the word *luxury* like
soap she would lather into bubbles on her hands or like
the taste of grapes she remembered cool and sweet.

The man saw her mother had a burn on the fleshy part
of her thumb opened the red and gold tin and said to
her mother to feel free to sample some.
Ironing her mother said.
Go ahead.
Her mother dipped a finger into the thick amber salve
and rubbed it onto the pink burn.
Hmph. That does feel better.
Good for cuts and scrapes too handy if you have
children and he looked at the girl and smiled.
The salve had some magical smell that filled her up
in a good way and made her feel saved and cured just
to smell it and look at it and know that it could heal
things. She thought of Saint Bernadette whose sore
leg was cured by magic water. This salve could surely
cure the scrapes on her knees or her elbows when she
hurt herself.

There was salve in a round flat tin of red and gold
and black on a shelf in the medicine cabinet in the
bathroom. Her mother also bought a green and
silver and black tin of ointment and slathered it on
the girl's neck when she was sick and had a sore
throat. *Ointment*. Her mother would safety pin one
of her father's scratchy grey wool work socks around

her neck to hold in the heat and the medicine. The ointment stung her nose when she breathed and she could feel the air in her lungs resting there like a stone.

Once the girl went to the medicine cabinet and cradled the tin of salve in her hand. The metal lip of the lid was tight but she finally managed to lift it off and touched her finger to the salve. She drew the letter "B" faintly on the smoothest surface of the salve. A "B" for St. Bernadette and then spread a small circle of ointment on her shin imagining herself as the saint in the movie. Now her lesions were cured. She wasn't sure exactly what lesions were but she was thankful she didn't have any in real life. She turned on the tap and made a bowl out of her hands to catch the water. It turned a milky white. A secret fountain like St. Bernadette's. The girl lifted her hands to her mouth as if to drink, but at the last second pressed the water into her face.

Once there was a man who came to the door trying to sell the girl's mother shiny silver pots and pans. The man with the pots and pans took off his hat and put his suitcase on the front step.
Ma'am if you'd just let me come in for ten minutes and demonstrate to you how these pots and pans could change your life and he looked at the girl and her sister and then glanced quickly through to the kitchen. I guarantee you'll be surprised at just how

well they cook. Wouldn't you like to cook better for your family? And the man looked down at the girl and her little sister. His smile looked like a cartoon snake.
I'm not going to buy them so you're wasting your time.
Well just give me ten minutes. Ten minutes.
I'm not buying anything.
Just ten minutes.
No I don't need any pots and pans I got a set for a wedding present.

The man stood in the door telling her mother a story. The girl thought it sounded like a fairy tale but he was talking very fast. He told her mother about a woman who had cooked in pots made of aluminum and how things like tomatoes or rhubarb would take off the top layer of the metal. Oh sure, he said, the pots seemed shinier but that metal would be in the tomatoes or the rhubarb and then when her children ate that food they would actually be eating: the metal.

Skate blades were metal. The girl thought of her father's skates in the back corner of the front hall closet. She had gone in there one day hoping to find a secret hiding place with treasure that would make her family rich so they could live in a big house in the west end like her father's boss but there were just the skates in the dusty corner. The toes were scuffed and the blades were spotted with rust. She had run her fingers over them but they weren't sharp at all.

Her mother would never want them eating metal.
But she remembered her father saying one night after supper those cheap aluminum pans would give him botulism or stomach cancer and her mother saying that was nonsense. Her father asked then how come every time she cooked rhubarb or tomatoes in those pots they always came out shinier and cleaner than they were before? The girl's mother slammed the door on the man with the pots and pans.
A man came to the door asking her mother if she needed any knives sharpened.
Come in then.

The girl followed her mother who had her arms crossed over her chest and her pink slippers clicking against her heels as she followed the pots and pan man whose feet left faint marks on the wood floor that followed him to the kitchen too and then the prints just disappeared. But when her mother let this man in she stood holding the door open with her back to the wall while he set down his black leather case. He took his shoes off in the porch and slipped them inside a black rubber that curved over the tops just a little bit.
A lady such as yourself needs the best knives, the sharpest knives the man said to her mother. The girl had never heard "such as yourself" spoken in the house before but it sounded very smart and made her mother sound so important and special.

The knife sharpener's socks had a blue diamond that had two narrow white lines through it. She could see the outline of his feet and watched him leaving tracks on the shining wood floor. The footprints disappearing in a path from the front door to the kitchen table as he made his way into their house. The girl thought of her father's socks. Thick wool, grey with white toes and heels and a narrow red stripe at the top. They reminded the girl of candy canes, but they weren't like that at all. When her father came home at night he took the folded newspapers from inside his boots, wet and shaped like all the footsteps he had taken that day, and threw them in the garbage. Gone. The day and his work. Pictures and stories thrown away.

The knife sharpener's voice was soft and ran along a quiet, even line. He opened a small black suitcase on the kitchen table and set down what looked like small swords on a piece of thick grey felt.

How many knives do you want me to sharpen? The man said and smiled at the girl's mother who put out the cigarette she had just lit in the little copper ashtray on the kitchen counter. She opened the cutlery drawer and the girl heard the jangle of forks, spoons and knives clanging against each other.

Only two that are worth it. A butcher knife and a bread knife. The paring knives I won't bother with. The man motioned for her mother to put the knives on the felt.

These are good knives he said.
Wedding gifts. One from my Mom and Dad and the other from my Uncle. A hunter.
How long have you been married?
Five years.
Are you from Edmonton?
No, moved here from Saskatchewan.
I'm not from here either. I'm a long way from home.

The girl was going to ask him where he was from but she soon forgot the question. The knife sharpener picked up one of his swords in one hand and held a knife in the other. Suddenly his hands and the knife and the sword were moving so quickly the girl couldn't tell where each started and ended and the noise was like skates on ice or the sound of her father's electric saw.
Why do you do that? The girl asked him.
This makes the blade so sharp. You know a dull knife is more dangerous than a sharp knife? See? I run the sharpener up both sides of the blade back and forth just so. Back and forth.
And he showed her how slowly and precisely as he moved the sword up one side of the blade and the other.
Now the second knife. He moved as quickly with the second as the first. A blur of hands and metal.
Let me try them now her mother said and taking one of the buns she had made yesterday she sliced it quickly and cleanly. Good she said.
I'm very glad you're happy.

A dollar, right?
No, I won't take anything this time. Next time I come back.
I don't have any other knives worth sharpening.
A knife in the kitchen is worth taking care of. How
would you do without them? I mean a woman such
as yourself.
Well at least let me get you a cup of coffee this time then.
That would be a pleasure. Thank you.
He gathered up his swords wrapping them in the felt
and tucked them gently in his suitcase. Snapped the
silver catches shut with a sound that made him seem
important. Made her mother seem important because
he had sharpened two knives and said he wouldn't
take anything. No charge her mother would tell her
father later when she showed off the almost-new knives
cutting buns for supper.
The guy didn't charge you nothing? What can you get
for nothing these days?
Well repeat business I guess. Maybe this is his new
territory.
The girl's father ripped a piece from the cleanly cut
bun cleaned his plate with it then crossed his knife
and fork on top of his yellow Melmac plate.

‹›‹›‹›

The knife sharpener came to the door another time. He looked the same and had the same soft voice but it was winter and cold and he wore a red scarf.
Come in the girl's mother said as soon as she opened the door.
I thought those other knives you had might need sharpening.
The girl saw her mother and the knife sharpener look right at each other and then her mother brush back the hair from her face and rub the back of her neck. Go watch TV the girl's mother said. The knife sharpener followed her mother to the kitchen. The girl thought she saw the man touch her mother's arm. So quick. Maybe it was a shadow.
The girl watched TV and her little sister slept. The light through the window was soft like the man's voice and her mother's. The blue screen curved out and warm toward the girl. She heard her mother and the knife sharpener laughing softly. He must be telling her a funny story.
Inside the TV a giant in a castle nudged some little chairs into rocking and she forgot how quiet the house was all of a sudden.

5

She ran her finger along the small triangle of ice that had collected in the bottom left corner of her bedroom window. Held her finger on an opaque ripple until it began to hurt. Put her finger to her cheek. Shivered.

It was the morning before Christmas Eve and the sun rose on her bedroom's side of the house. The light seemed lazy against her window against the cold colour made by the sun on glass and ice.

She watched as the neighbour Mr. Vanderveen opened his front door how cold the silver handle must be how cold and stiff the thick silver hinges how cold the silent silver swan stuck forever in the middle of screen. A fairy tale about seven swans and the seven sweaters their sister would knit them while not talking for seven years. The sweaters and her silence would set those swans free but the story of the cold silver swan on the neighbour's door might never start and might never end.

As Mr. Vanderveen shut the door behind him it was hard to tell where the warm of the house and the cold of outside started and ended. For a moment white vapour was caught behind him in two great wings. Maybe the swan trying to fly away from the door the girl thought. Mr. Vanderveen patted the side of his brown tweed coat his leather gloves peaking from his sleeves like dark brown wing tips. His face was hidden by the brim of his grey hat. It had a small red feather sticking out of the band. The girl saw his dog Tatters jump off the bottom step and the puffs of Mr. Vanderveen's breath as the dog jumped rocking-horse style on the cold sidewalk. Then opening his gate of white sticks the two turned down the street walking quickly through the soft white air.

She liked that at this time of year air stopped being invisible. The tiny specks of ice floated over the bare trees in their dancer poses arching over the street and played around the straight lines of the electrical wires held tight over the street by the power poles. She envied the trees being able to be outside in the cold but she felt sorry for them too because they couldn't move no matter how hard they tried. They were just stuck in the same spot all the time. Like the swan on the neighbour's door.

When she drew a picture of her house it also included the trees in a row on the street in front of her house and the street lights curving watchful at night with straight lines from the round lights shining soft and saying quiet we will keep you safe and a row of power poles in the alley with wires running from one to the other. Sometimes she drew birds red or blue sitting on the black lines. Never more than three birds. It took too long to draw more. Beaks tiny eyes feet and claws clutching the wire.

She knew the other houses on the street and now she knew some of the people in them. Her friend across the alley. She had sisters and brothers and they all walked to their church on the corner every Sunday. Then the neighbours on the left side of their house. They had children but they were all grown up and they were all alone except for Tatters.

Her house was on the corner or maybe the end of the street depending which way you were walking. She thought the house was big with its wood floors that shone different shapes at her throughout the day as the sun circled around the house. A special golden dance around their corner house at the end of her street.

Her house and her street were in Santa Rosa. She thought the name of her neighbourhood sounded so beautiful and so faraway. But it wasn't far away at all. It was also the name of the big street Santa Rosa Avenue down past the grocery store. The big street her family drove on when they were on their way to somewhere. It was the name of the grocery store. It was the name of the skating rink. It was the name of the place they lived and she was here. But she wouldn't be here this Christmas. This Christmas they were going to Saskatchewan. Going back home to Saskatchewan her mother always said. Back to her grandmother's house. Back to her mother's home.

The girl heard her mother on the phone in the kitchen. Asking to talk to herself. It seemed so strange to hear her mother say her own name. The girl thought it strange to hear her mother's name in the house at all. She called her Mom her sister called her Mom in her tiny voice but her father hardly ever said her mother's name.

Call and ask for yourself. Call and ask for yourself so I know you're coming her grandmother would tell her mother.
Call and ask for yourself. Call and ask for yourself just before you're leaving so I know when to expect you.
Why would you ask for yourself? the girl had asked. You know you're here not at Gramma's yet.
You phone long distance and ask for yourself person-to-person. Then since the person you ask for isn't there you don't get charged for the call.

The girl didn't quite understand but thought it must be right if her mother did it. Saving money was good.

This morning the girl's mother was asking for herself. That was the magic trick of the person-to-person call. They were going back to Saskatchewan.

Her mother was calling her grandmother at the house in town because her aunt and uncle had moved into the house on the farm. Her mother was asking to speak to herself. Now her grandmother knew they were coming. It was all set. They were really going back to Saskatchewan this Christmas. Her mother hung up the phone the same way she hung coats on the hooks at the back door and she wore the happiest face she had worn in a long time.

Yes today was the day before Christmas Eve.

The girl had gotten up early. As soon as she opened her eyes she could smell the Christmas tree in every part of the house even when she was in bed. She closed her eyes again. The smell was still there. She knelt on her bed in front of her bedroom window. She could see the red lights dotting the roof next door through the steam at the top of her window.

She flicked off the chenille bedspread and shivered when her feet touched the floor. She hurried to the corner of the living room and knelt before the tree her nightgown stretching taut pulling from her shoulders to her knees. She could feel the neck opening pressing a straight line at the top of her spine as she reached around the back of the tree to plug in the lights. There. She leaned back into the light of the winter morning dark. Blue red green teardrops spilling from every branch. An ornament on every branch and every one was her favourite. Her face reflected back at her in the shiny red and blue globes. The smaller decorations seemed to be dusted with snow pale and quiet.

The girl heard the radio faint in the kitchen. *Have a holly jolly Christmas* . . . that was one of her mother's favourite Christmas songs and she liked it too. It made her feel so happy almost as happy as Jingle Bells when she shouted *Hey!* as loud as she could and no one got mad at her for yelling. There were some sad things about Christmas too she knew like the story of the little match girl which her mother had read to her. The girl was glad she had a mother and father and didn't have to sell matches or knives or Watkins salves.

Yes her father said he was just going to work until lunch. Last night the girl heard him tell her mother he only had to check up on the basement they poured yesterday god damn it I hate pouring concrete in this cold he said.

So he would come home they would load up the car her mother would put sandwiches she had wrapped in wax paper in a big brown paper bag. They would hit the road. The girl loved it when her father said that. He would say let's hit the road as they backed out of the driveway and he would look behind him out the back window with a cigarette in his mouth and his arm on the front seat and smile down at her in the back seat.

Her mother had been getting ready for this trip all week. Making sure there wasn't too much food in the fridge so it wouldn't spoil when they were gone a few days. Washing clothes so the house smelled like Christmas tree and soap and outside.

They hadn't been to Saskatchewan since her birthday in the spring. Her mother hadn't taken so much time to get ready for that trip. The girl didn't remember her mother talking about it and there were no person-to-person calls that time. Her mother put clothes in their hard brown suitcase and snapped it shut. There were dirty clothes in the basket. Told her they had to hurry but the girl wasn't sure why. Her mother called a taxi that came to take the girl her mother and her sister to the train station downtown. The girl's father didn't come.

The three of them took the train to Saskatchewan that trip to her grandmother's house in town and had stayed long enough that her mother had to wash clothes. Stayed long enough that they had the girl's birthday at her grandmother's. Take a picture. Squinting into the sun she had held up a birthday cake with white icing and five red and candy cane striped candles. Another picture. Squinting into the sun she held up a hand puppet bumblebee she had gotten for a present. Picture. Her favourite light blue dress.

That trip seemed like a long time ago and her mother had seemed sad even though she said she was not homesick anymore. The girl's father never phoned her mother that trip. Not even person-to-person to ask for himself. Her mother never phoned him either. The girl pretended not to hear her mother talking to her grandmother at the kitchen table early in the morning. The pump at the sink ticking with a drip of water and the plastic curtain on the window over the sink puffing in and out from the screen like bubble gum from the girl's mouth and the smoke from her mother's and grandmother's cigarettes being pulled toward the window and out into the fresh air.
I'm not calling him. I'll see how long it takes for him to make a move. If he ever does.
And her grandmother saying
Well what are you going to do then?
I know what I'd do if I didn't have two kids the girl's mother said.

When the girl asked her mother what was wrong she looked really surprised and just about to take a puff of her cigarette dropped it on the floor.
Jesus! She quickly picked it up from the filter red sparks dropping like little fireworks from the tip skittering over the circle and tic-tac-toe shapes on the linoleum floor.
Nothing's wrong.
But the girl's mother didn't look at her when she said it.

Didn't look at her grandmother when she said it. The girl didn't know what was wrong but it was something. She hoped her father would call person-to-person. He never did. He just showed up in the car early Saturday morning laughed and said Well here I am. Come on I'm taking you home. The girl's parents sat outside in the car in the backyard of her grandmother's house in town for a long time smoking and talking. The girl's grandmother didn't even look at them when she went to slowly hang out sheets and pillowcases on the clothesline. They flapped like the wings of giant angels back and forth beside the car until the girl's parents just looked silly and unimportant sitting out there covered with a bright blue sky and shooed away by white sheets and pillowcases. They both came back into the house. The girl her sister and her mother were packed and gone before lunch.

We'll get something to eat in North Battleford the girl's father had said.

The girl's mother had hugged her grandmother longer than she had ever seen her hug anyone before. Even though the girl's grandmother said it quietly the girl heard it anyway.

Don't let things get you down.

She gave the girl and her sister a long hug and called them both her little dollies. The girl looked out the back window and waved as if she would never see her grandmother again and her grandmother blew her a kiss and the girl imagined that the sheets and pillowcases flapping on the clothesline passed the kiss along their wings to catch her in the backseat of the car. She looked out the back window until her father turned the corner and she couldn't see her grandmother anymore.

Her father drove down Main Street past the café and said Wonder if they ever got around to changing the songs on the jukebox. Eh? What do you think? Eh?
He laughed and looked over at the girl's mother. He held the steering wheel with one hand reached across to take a cigarette package from the left pocket of his shirt.
Her mother just stared out the window.
Some things never change I guess she said and didn't look at the girl's father when she said it.
Then they were over the railroad tracks turning on to the highway with sky all around them driving home. The wind rushing past the car and rumbling into the windows and smelling like dirt after it rains and cut grass and every now and then just for a second the faint scent of pine from the little green Christmas tree dancing back and forth from the rear view mirror.

Now the Christmas tree was set up straight in the living room. The whole house smelled like a Christmas tree and soap from the clothes and outside when her mother brought the clothes in still stiff and frozen from the clothesline in the backyard.

The girl thought of her grandmother waving to her that day with the sheets and pillowcases waving too. She remembered her grandmother hanging clothes out on the line pretending not to see her mother and father in the car. How happy her grandmother would be to see them this Christmas.

The girl's mother was just like her grandmother this past week hanging clothes out on the clothesline in their backyard. The clothesline was a straight line that ran from the back porch to the garage but in winter it disappeared in the cold white air. Her mother hung towels and sheets with bare hands so she could open and snap closed the clothespins.
So cold. These clothes were not like huge wings but like giant icicles or the shapes of flags or the shapes of upside-down hanging people or the shapes of feet running away from their yard to Santa Rosa Avenue.

Her mother brought a basket of clothes up from the dirt cellar wet and pressed into flat pieces that folded into and out of themselves like fans. Her mother put on the work boots the girl's father wore in summer not bothering to do up the laces and then put on her coat with flecks of brown and black and grey and did up the big brown buttons. Under the coat she wore the girl's father's long grey underwear and a plaid shirt of the girl's father as well. Out the back door carrying the clothes and hanging them on the line. She was sure she saw the ghost of each of them in the house fly away from the clothesline into the cold winter air and past the back yard and into the neighbourhood disappearing to somewhere just as happy. It was Christmas.

And when her mother brought the clothes back inside they were frozen hard and cold even if they felt like they were dry already. The past few days getting ready for the trip her mother had strung clotheslines up inside the house too and hung the clothes on the inside lines. The girl's skipping ropes were suspended from nails in the corners of the windows like strings of peppermint candy canes criss-crossing the living room and the dining room. She danced underneath and if she tried hard she could touch the bottom of each piece of clothing and be part of that person in her family. Her mother's favourite and best white blouse with the long cuffs and big sleeves big collar and bow at the neck her father's red plaid work shirt and the girl's own red velveteen jumper her best and favourite. It was like another part of herself. She would wear that jumper on Christmas day. She danced and made her arms a circle above her head and tried to turn in the air as she jumped. A skater or a ballerina. She pictured herself so pretty with Christmas songs in the background and her parents opening presents and kissing each other and saying I love you and I love you too like the Christmas people on television. But her mother told her stop that all the lines would fall down on them and the clothes would get dirty and she wasn't washing all over again.

The girl turned from the Christmas tree in the corner of the living room to the TV and then back to the tree as her mother ironed clothes and folded them into a suitcase. The girl thought the Christmas tree was the most magical thing and liked to kneel close to it. She would run her fingers softly through the silver strands of tinsel hanging from the branches and imagine they really were icicles as cold as the ice on the corner of her bedroom window. She stared into the round ornaments and saw her face reflected curving into the brightness of shiny red or blue and showing her everything that was happening behind her without her having to even turn around. Her sister asleep on the couch her mother holding a cigarette between her fingers as she swept the floor with the scratchy witch broom. She couldn't see her father of course because he was at work but he would be home soon and then they would go.

The light was cold bright coming in the windows. The girl's mother looked out the kitchen window to the empty driveway the black extension cord curving in the snow the plug waiting for their car. The girl told her mother she was getting hungry. Her mother said she was always hungry.

The girl skipped to the kitchen table because all the clotheslines inside had been taken down. The clothes were put away or packed to go.

Everything just seemed happier at Christmas. Even the dishes the Melmac plates and cups looked as if colour had been poured onto the kitchen table pink yellow toffee and taken the shapes of the dishes. They were bright and hard plastic and could take whatever you kids dish out that's what her mother always said.

Her mother had made her soup that had letters of the alphabet in it. She put the empty can in the garbage under the kitchen sink and said that would have to be taken out before they left. Her mother said for them not to get dirty and went to the bedroom. The girl scooped up letters from her bowl a W or it could be M. That was the best thing about those two letters it just depended on how you looked at it. How things were turned around. She scooped up a broken M. It twisted on her spoon. That letter was nothing now just broken lines. The girl took the pile of four crackers beside the bowl and crushed them into the soup and let them get soft and red. Even the soup was a Christmas colour.

The girl heard their heavy suitcase snap shut. The soft thud of her mother's footsteps as she put the suitcase by the back door. She lit a cigarette and leaned against the counter by the sink. She looked out the window and was forgetting to smoke her cigarette.

The girl finished the soup and her mother took the bowl right away rinsed it dried it and put it back in the cupboard. There was nothing in the sink except the damp dishcloth folded over the dripping faucet.

Go watch TV if you want she told the girl. And the girl sat in front of the TV as it started getting dark and she plugged in the Christmas tree lights and they shone colour from the corner of the living room and she thought she knew what tidings of comfort and joy meant. Her sister woke up and her Dad wasn't home.

The news came on and then there was the noise of the back door opening and a rush of cold into the house. She heard her father laughing louder than she had ever heard him laugh before. He was home now and finally they could go. But another man's voice was laughing too. She ran to the kitchen. A man she didn't know was trying to hold the back door open as he dragged her father inside. The back porch light shone hard white into the wings of cold vapour following her father and the man into the house. Her father was still laughing and the girl saw each sound harden in the air like ice. Even though her father was laughing he didn't seem really happy. This kind of happy scared her.

The man was trying to lift her father up the three back stairs into the kitchen. Her father couldn't stand and was trying to grab the railing. The girl just stood in the middle of the kitchen. She was afraid. Afraid for her father afraid of her father. She had seen a program on TV about a doctor whose patient had been paralyzed in a car crash. She started to cry and could only stand there. Her body felt covered with ice. The inside of her mouth began to hurt as if she had eaten too much ice cream too fast. The cold spread to the back of her eyes to the top of her head. She didn't know what to do with her hands so she left the tears alone. She was frozen. Like the sound of her father's laughter still trapped in the cold outside the back door.

Are you turning paralyzed Dad?

The man and the girl's father both laughed harder but the girl saw her mother start to cry without making any noise. The man and the girl's father didn't notice.

The man heaved her father up the last stair with him still trying to grab for the railing her father's green parka flapping open the zipper clicking against the railing. He flopped on to the kitchen floor and sat propped against the wall with his legs straight out and his work boots still on. The snow started to melt on to the kitchen floor and his boots were smearing water as he tried to brace himself against the wall so he could stand. The man and her father couldn't seem to stop laughing. Maybe her father hadn't gone paralyzed after all.

The girl recognized the shape of the lights driving into the backyard.
I had one of the guys drive your car here for you the man said to her father not even looking at the girl's mother. He went back outside took the keys from the person who drove their car into the driveway and brought them back in. The man simply said Keys? and handed them to the girl's mother. The man slammed the door as he left the cold air staying in the back porch as if the thought of him was still there. For a second the house was still and quiet. So quiet the girl just stood there. She could still smell the Christmas tree in the living room and thought she could hear the colour of the Christmas lights moving through the glass and through the green wire that linked all the lights together. There was a moment of dead air on the TV.

The girl's mother pulled at her father trying to get him up off the floor and he was whistling and singing and laughing as he leaned on her in the door of their bedroom. He took off his work boots and jacket and just crawled into bed with his clothes on. The girl stood at the bedroom door.

They never even change the songs in the goddamn café he said. The songs never change and he laughed gathering the pillow with his arms as if it were a person or something. He finally pushed his head into a spot on the pillow and was quiet then. The girl's mother shut the door and didn't even seem worried or mad. The girl thought she might look like she was trying not to cry.

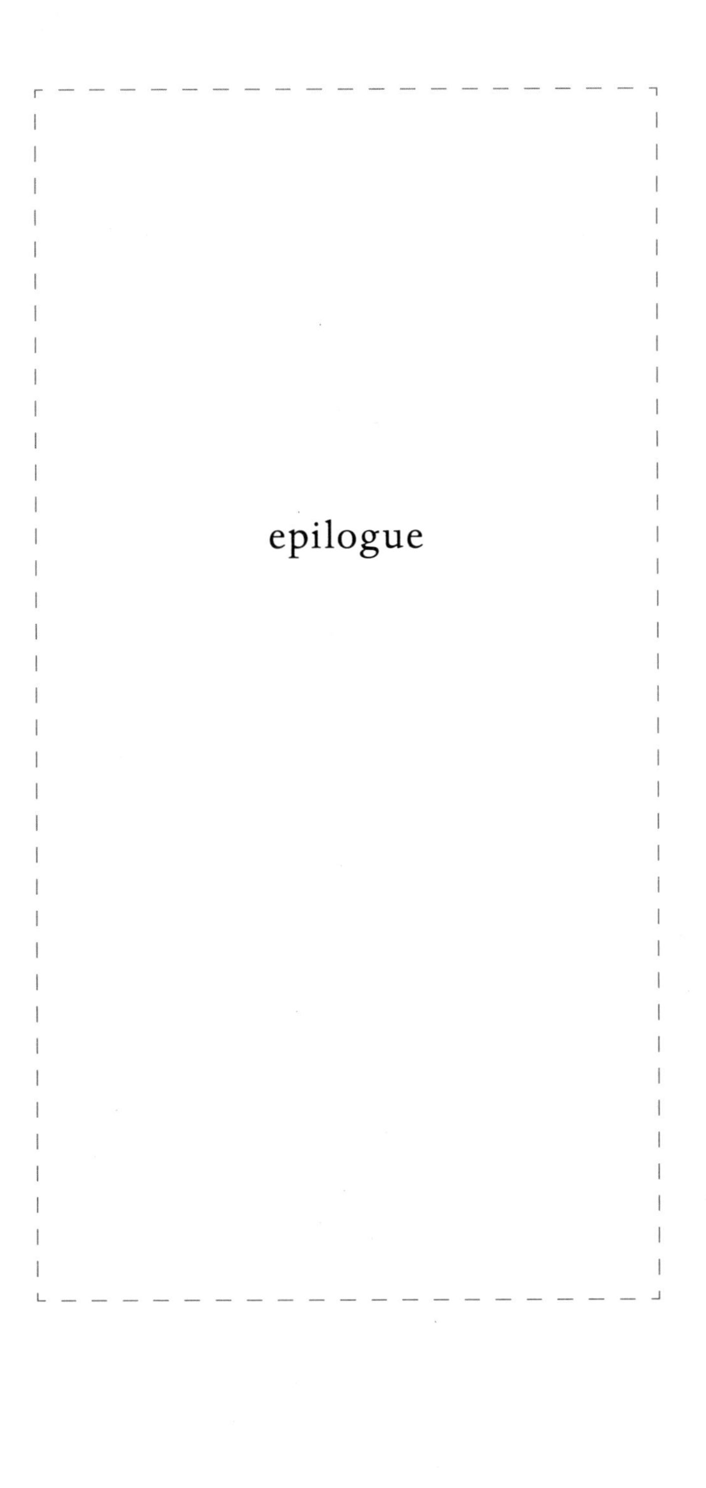

epilogue

The sky was red.

Colour poured through the window red and endless variations of. The very heart of the colour the very purpose of what touched the skin on her face the taste on her tongue that sensation of cinnamon nutmeg pepper came right through the cold glass and cast its pigment on her and every wall every piece of furniture every piece of clothing every dish and cup in the house and in some way transformed it.

The sky was a red that sparked and snapped against the night. A red that moved in a dancer's rhythm trailing ribbons of white and pink in the frozen cold. She had never seen anything like it.

She shivered her reaction to the colour catching her off guard. Her own skin hurt surprising her underneath her sweater. She looked down and touching the knitted rows of wool they changed from blue to red. The brightness drew her back to the sky in disbelief.
A dream.

MomMom come quick come and see

Her mother running up the cellar steps as quickly as she could the tone of her daughter's voice telling her she must be hurt.

What? What is it?

All the girl was able to do was point at the kitchen window.

What is it?

Her mother looked up at the red its colour crackled its hue and the trail it left as it shook itself out in slow motion. She looked up at the red that had become the sky above her house and could say nothing. She closed her eyes tight and opened them again expecting to see what she always saw at this time of night at this time of year in this room of the house a blue-black sky the same colour as her daughter's favourite crayon.

But she knew she would never see anything like this again. She opened her eyes wider. The sky was on fire.

Then looked her daughter straight in the eye laughed out loud and embraced her.

Now that is something she said.

The girl laughed too. She had not heard her mother laugh like that in a long long time. She could not remember since when. She thought it might have been never and held on to her with her eyes closed and her face smashed into the scratch of her mother's sweater. She thought this will be another colour for me to put on paper and think on my tongue. This red sky her mother laughing this red will make an impression like nothing else so far. I know the perfect thing. I know what I need to do to remember this feeling. I know how I can hold it in my hand.

The sky continued in that state of red for what seemed hours and the girl and her mother just stayed at the window their breath creating small rings of vapour. They just stayed and watched. Stayed silent and watched.

Quickly the noise and colour that had made her feel needles all over her skin was gone.

Will it come back Mom?
Oh I don't know. If it does it won't be for a very long time. We might not even be here to see it she said.

Then smiled. Tightened her sweater around herself and turned toward the cellar door opening from the kitchen floor to a dirt basement. She turned her back on the red and descended back into the cellar. The slosh of the washing machine and the sound of her mother's feet click click click down the skeleton stairs.

She felt a love for her mother in that moment that she would return to at other times and other places. It would be what she would remember about that night.

The girl went to bed that night feeling as if she had bathed in red. Her skin electrified by the colour of the sky.

In a few hours this day would be gone.

One day Santa Rosa would be gone too.

acknowledgements

As always, thank you John for your infinite patience and support.

Eamon and Brendan—thank you both for being such an inspiration to me.

Thanks to *Descant* which published a version of a portion of this novel in Volume 34, Issue 1 (Spring 2003).

Some parts of this novel began in University of Alberta creative writing classes in which I participated—thanks to T. Wharton and my fellow students for their feedback.

Finally, thanks to Doug Barbour, Andrew Wilmot, Paul Matwychuk and designer Natalie Olsen for their belief in this book and their sensitivity to my vision.

I would like to acknowledge the music and films mentioned in this novel:

Jimmy Williams and Larry Harrison, "(You Don't Know) How Glad I Am," (performed by Nancy Wilson) Capitol Records, 1964.

The Song of Bernadette, Dir. Henry King, starring Jennifer Jones, Twentieth Century Fox, 1943.

Joan of Arc, Dir. Victor Fleming, starring Ingrid Bergman, Sierra Pictures, 1948.

Gerry Marsden, "Ferry Cross the Mersey," Columbia (EMI), 1964.

Johnny Marks, "A Holly Jolly Christmas," performed by Burl Ives, MCA Records, 1965.

Santa Rosa is Wendy McGrath's second novel.

Her first novel, *Recurring Fictions,* was published in 2002 by the University of Alberta Press, and her first collection of poems, *common place ecstasies,* was published by Beach Holme Publishing in 2000.

McGrath has numerous poetry, fiction and nonfiction publication and broadcast credits.

She has teamed with Edmonton printmaker and U of A professor emeritus Walter Jule in collaborative exhibitions of prints and poetry. These have evolved into the text/print/multimedia project, *A Revision of Forward.*